My
Halloween
Boyfriend

Other Young Yearling Books You Will Enjoy:

Yearling Books/Young Yearlings/Yearling Classics are designed especially to entertain and enlighten young people. Patricia Reilly Giff, consultant to this series, received the bachelor's degree from Marymount College. She holds the master's degree in history from St. John's University, and a Professional Diploma in Reading from Hofstra University. She was a teacher and reading consultant for many years, and is the author of numerous books for young readers.

For a complete listing of all Yearling titles, write to
Dell Readers Service, P.O. Box 1045,
South Holland, IL 60473.

THE
CREEPY
CREATURE
CLUB

My
Halloween
Boyfriend

◆

Stephen Mooser

Illustrated by George Ulrich

A YOUNG YEARLING BOOK

Published by
Dell Publishing
a division of
Bantam Doubleday Dell Publishing Group, Inc.
666 Fifth Avenue
New York, New York 10103

ISBN: 0-440-40231-X

Printed in the United States of America

October 1989

10 9 8 7 6 5 4 3 2

W

For Ashley and Brett Englander

Contents

Chapter 1

◆

A Creature in the Classroom

Monday Morning.

Jody Grimes was late to class.

Down the hall she walked. Slowly. Her head was down. Her stomach hurt.

"I wish I could be somewhere, anywhere else," she said to herself. "School stinks."

At last she came to Room 6. She took a deep breath and reached into the big pocket on the side of her dress. Her hand grabbed hold of her good-luck charm, a rubber four-leaf clover. She gave it a squeeze and wished for a good day.

Then, with a sigh, she opened the door.

"Yeow! Yikes! A monster!" she screamed. Her curly black hair nearly straightened itself out. "Yeeeeeow!"

There was a monster in Ms. Hatfield's classroom. A tall, ugly monster. With a green, warty face. And a big red nose, split down the middle.

"Jody, please," said the monster. The creature pulled off its mask. "Don't be scared. It's only me, Ms. Hatfield."

Jody gulped. It was her teacher, dressed up. Everyone in the class was laughing.

"Did you forget? Halloween is this Friday," said Ms. Hatfield. "I was showing the class my Halloween costume."

Jody put a hand on her heart. "Whew!" She took a deep breath and tried to act calm. "Monsters usually don't scare me. I see them all the time at the Creepy Creature Club. But you surprised me. I didn't expect to find a monster in class."

"This week you'll see lots of monsters," said Ms. Hatfield. "Halloween is coming." She smiled and pointed. "Please take your seat."

Jody went to her desk. She looked over at Henry Potter. "Wow!" she said. "That was scary."

Like Jody, Henry was in the Creepy Creature Club. It was a club for people who liked monsters. They went to monster movies, collected monster trading cards, and even met in a place decorated like a haunted house.

Henry leaned his long, thin body across the aisle.

"I was at the joke shop yesterday. You should see what I bought," he whispered. As usual, Henry's hair was sticking up in back. Like a feather.

Jody waved him away. "Please. I'm real nervous right now. All kinds of things are bothering me. I just want to be left alone."

"This thing is great," said Henry. "Believe me. You'll love it."

"Not now," she said. "I need to relax. Please."

Jody's heart was still pounding.

"I wish I was still at home," she thought to herself. "Or sitting by a little river, talking to Tommy Lee Turner."

Tommy Lee Turner was the star of *My Zombie Boyfriend.* Jody's parents thought it was the dumbest show on TV. But Jody thought it was the best. Tuesday night at eight. She never missed it. Last night she had even written Tommy a letter. "Dear Tommy," it began. "How did you get to be a TV star? I want to be one too. Do you

4

know why? Because TV stars don't have to go to school. Write back soon. Real soon. Before grades come out. Your friend, Jody."

While Jody was daydreaming, Henry put something on the back of her hand.

"Check this out," he said.

Jody opened her eyes.

"Yeeow!" she screamed. "A spider!"

The thing on her hand, a big hairy ball, went flying.

"Jody! It's just a fake," said Henry. He shot a look at Ms. Hatfield. "It's from the joke shop. Pretty neat, huh?"

Jody glared at Henry. She felt like stuffing the spider up his nose.

Ms. Hatfield peered over her glasses. "Jody, is everything all right?"

Jody forced a smile. "Just practicing my screaming," she said. "For Halloween."

Ms. Hatfield put a finger to her lips. "Next time, dear, please not so loud."

Behind her, Jody heard someone laughing. It was Angie Dobbs.

Angie belonged to the Sharks. The Sharks were a club. A club of bullies. The Sharks and the Creepy Creatures didn't like each other. Not one bit.

5

Angie said, "Scared? I thought Creepy Creatures never got scared."

Jody turned around. "Shut up, smarty pants!"

Angie stuck out her tongue. Her stringy hair hung down to her shoulders. It looked like a dirty brown waterfall.

"I'd rather be a smarty pants than what you are," she said.

"And just what is that?" said Jody.

"A dummy pants," whispered Angie, grinning. "You get the worst grades in class."

"Go eat a bug," whispered Jody. She stared at her desk.

Dummy pants! The words hurt.

"I am dumb," she thought. "And everyone knows it."

Chapter 2

◆

The Mind Reader

At the end of the day Ms. Hatfield had some exciting news.

"On Friday everyone should wear a costume. The best costume will win a prize," she said.

"A prize!" said Henry. "Give it to me now. I'll have the best one for sure."

Everyone laughed. Henry was always bragging.

"Wait," said Ms. Hatfield. She raised her hand for silence. "There's more."

Ms. Hatfield smiled. "On Friday a TV show is coming to our class. We're going to be on television."

"TV!" said little Melvin Purdy. His brown eyes were round as pie pans. "Really?"

"Yes, really," said Ms. Hatfield. She winked. "Some of you may soon be stars."

"What is the name of the show?" asked Henry.

"You'll find out on Friday," said Ms. Hatfield. "It's all part of the surprise prize. The prize for the best costume."

Just then the bell rang. Everyone leapt up. In a rush they grabbed their books and tumbled toward the door.

"Jody!" shouted Ms. Hatfield. "Wait. I want to see you."

Jody stopped. She waited for the classroom to empty. Then she walked slowly up to Ms. Hatfield's desk. Her stomach started to tighten up. She put her hand in her pocket and squeezed her rubber four-leaf clover. She hoped she wasn't about to get in trouble.

"Jody, you didn't do your book report last week," said Ms. Hatfield. "Do you have it?"

Jody looked down. She fiddled with her sleeve. "No. I'm sorry. It's going to be late."

Ms. Hatfield shook her head. "Jody, you're always late. And sometimes you don't do your work at all. If you don't get a report to me by Friday I'll have to call your parents."

8

Jody gulped. "Really?"

"In fact, if you don't improve you may have to stay back next year. Repeat the class."

"Oh, no. Please. Not that," said Jody.

"Then do your book report," said Ms. Hatfield. "You're a smart girl. I know you can do it."

Jody looked up into Ms. Hatfield's round face. "I'll try," she said. She wished that there was no such thing as school. She wished that it could be summer vacation. Forever.

"Don't just say you'll try," said Ms. Hatfield. "Say you'll do it."

Jody smiled. "I promise."

"I know you can do it," said Ms. Hatfield. She patted Jody on the shoulder. "Now go. Run on home."

Rosa Dorado was waiting for Jody in the hall. Rosa was Jody's best friend.

"You got in trouble, didn't you?" said Rosa.

Jody nodded.

"I knew it. And it was all because you didn't do your book report. Right?"

Jody gasped. "How did you know?"

Rosa smiled and held up a little red book.

"Simple. Last week I did my book report on this."

Jody squinted. She read off the words on the book's cover: *How to Read Minds and Tell the Future.*

"You mean you read Ms. Hatfield's mind?"

"Not exactly," said Rosa. "Actually, I saw a note on Ms. Hatfield's desk. It said, 'See Jody. Book report. Late!!!' " She slapped the book into the palm of her hand. "But I have been practicing. One of these days I really will be able to read minds."

Together they walked down the hall and out of the school.

"What did Ms. Hatfield say?" asked Rosa.

"She said my report was due on Friday. If I don't do it I might have to stay back a year."

"You'd better do that report," said Rosa.

Jody laughed. "Don't worry. I'm going to."

"I'm sure that you are," said Rosa. She looked down at her book. "In fact, I predict it."

Chapter 3

◆

The Best Clubhouse Anywhere

"**W**ho's there?" asked Henry from behind the door of the Creepy Creature clubhouse. The clubhouse was in Rosa Dorado's garage. Even Rosa had to give the secret knock.

"It's Frank," said Rosa.

"Frank who?"

"Frank N. Stein," said Jody. "Let us in."

"Enter, if you dare," said Henry, opening the door.

As Rosa and Jody walked past, Henry winked.

"Handsome Henry welcomes you to his home, sweet haunted home," he said. "Please, make yourselves uncomfortable."

Rosa and Jody looked at each other. They

giggled. Henry was not the world's best-looking boy. Only the world's best bragger.

"Look what I just put up," he said. "The scariest skeleton on earth."

Jody looked up at the ceiling. A big plastic skeleton hung over a long green couch. The skeleton's teeth were red.

Everyone agreed the Creepy Creatures had the best clubhouse anywhere. Monster-movie posters covered the walls. Big rubber spiders dangled from the ceiling. And on the back table were three plastic skulls.

Most of the nine kids in the club were already there. Some were standing around. Some were sitting on the couch. And some were reading monster magazines.

Jody went off by herself. She sat down in a corner and opened her backpack. Then she took out a copy of *Monster Madness* magazine. It was the newest issue. She could hardly wait to read it. That's because Tommy Lee Turner was on the cover. He was dressed up like the Zombie Boyfriend, all in rags and blood except for a pair of white gloves.

Just then Rosa clapped her hands. "Attention," she said. "Time to start the meeting."

Everyone stopped what they were doing. Everyone but Jody. "Ah," she sighed, turn-

13

ing a page. "I could read about Tommy Lee Turner all day."

"Today we are going to look into some-one's brain," said Rosa. She ran a hand through her long black hair. "As you know, I've been studying mind reading. I think this might be a good time to try it out."

"Whose mind do you want to read?" asked Melvin. He swallowed. "This won't be scary, will it?"

"Melvin, don't be a jellyfish. Of course this won't be scary. We're just looking into one brain: Ms. Hatfield's."

"Our teacher!" said Henry. "Why her?"

"I want to know what the secret prize is," said Rosa. "The prize for the best costume."

Henry said, "Maybe it will be a Hallow-een pumpkin."

"Or maybe a candy heart," said Melvin.

Rosa rolled her big brown eyes. "Melvin, a heart is for Valentine's Day. This is Hal-loween week."

"Maybe it has something to do with that TV show she talked about," said Henry. "Ms. Hatfield wouldn't say which one it was."

Rosa pointed at Henry. "You may be right. But what show?"

"A Halloween show," said Henry. He was

15

feeling pretty smart. "Why else would she want us to dress up?"

Rosa put a hand on her forehead. She closed her eyes. Tight.

"Come on, everybody. Think. If we can read Ms. Hatfield's mind we can get the name of the show."

The room fell silent. Everyone was trying hard to peek inside Ms. Hatfield's brain.

After a minute Jody popped to her feet. "I've got it!" she said. "I know what show is coming!"

"Amazing!" said Rosa. "Jody has read our teacher's mind."

"Not quite," said Jody. She walked toward Rosa. "I read something, but it wasn't a mind."

"What was it?" asked Rosa.

"It was *Monster Madness*," said Jody. She waved the magazine in Rosa's face. "The answer, my friend, is right here."

Chapter 4

The Contest

"**L**ook," said Jody. She opened the magazine and pointed to a page. "Here is Ms. Hatfield's special prize."

Melvin Purdy leaned forward and squinted.

"All I see is a picture of Tommy Lee Turner. Is he the prize?"

"No, silly," said Jody. She handed the magazine to Melvin. "Go on. Read what it says under the picture."

Melvin cleared his throat.

" 'Dress like a zombie and win a part on *My Zombie Boyfriend,*' " said Melvin, reading. " 'On Halloween, Tommy Lee Turner will be out looking for great zombie costumes. He could be anywhere in the country. If he likes your costume you could win first prize.' "

17

"And first prize is a part on his show," said Jody. She was so excited she was bouncing up and down. "Don't you see? *My Zombie Boyfriend* is the surprise TV show coming to our class!"

"That would be exciting," said Henry.

"It would be—if it were true," said Rosa. "Face it. No big star would pick our school."

"Why wouldn't he?" said Jody. "He has to go somewhere." She put a hand on her heart. "Oh! I can't believe it! Tommy Lee Turner!"

"Sounds like you want to win the contest," said Rosa. "Am I right? Are you going to dress like a zombie on Friday?"

"Of course I am," said Jody. "I want to be a star. Don't you?"

"It might be fun."

"Fun? It would be great!" said Jody. She rubbed her hands together and wiggled her eyebrows. "For the rest of this week I'm going to do nothing but work on my costume. When I'm done I'll be the best zombie in the whole country."

Rosa pointed a finger at Jody. "Don't forget about your book report. That's due on Friday too."

Jody waved her hand at Rosa. "Book report? Don't make me laugh!"

"But what about Ms. Hatfield?" said Rosa.

"I don't care about Ms. Hatfield," said Jody. She did a little dance. "After Friday I won't be in school anymore. Or even here in River City."

Henry's mouth flopped open. "You won't? Where will you be?"

"Hollywood," said Jody. She sighed and looked up at the ceiling. "Silly boy. Don't you know anything? That's where all the stars live."

Chapter 5

◆

Zombies on Parade

Tuesday.

Jody was in class, but she really wasn't in school. Only her body was there. Her mind was somewhere else.

Probably in Hollywood.

During geography, Rosa saw that Jody had a magazine hidden inside her book.

Instead of studying the map of Europe she was reading about Tommy Lee Turner.

"Jody!" whispered Rosa. "You're going to get in trouble."

Jody smiled. Rosa wasn't sure, but it looked as if Jody was wearing lipstick. And maybe some eye shadow too.

Rosa shook her head. "If you don't do

your schoolwork you're going to be something besides a star," she said.

"Oh, yeah, what's that?" whispered Jody.

"A stay-back," said Rosa.

After school Henry met Rosa in the hallway. Henry thought Rosa was the prettiest girl in the world. He liked spending time with her. Even if it was just for a stroll down the hall.

"Is Jody doing her report?" he asked.

"No, and I don't think she will either," said Rosa.

"Why do you think that?" asked Henry.

Rosa tapped her forehead. "I've been concentrating. Trying to see inside Jody's brain," she said.

"And?" said Henry.

Rosa shrugged her shoulders. "It doesn't look good. I think she's going to leave school."

"Maybe she really will get a part on TV," said Henry. "Then she wouldn't have to go to school."

"You have to be smart to be on TV," said Rosa. "Anyone who quits school isn't very smart."

As they passed by the library Rosa saw something that stopped her cold.

"I don't believe it. That looks like Jody, studying," she said.

Rosa and Henry stuck their heads into the library. Sure enough, it was Jody Grimes. She was seated at a table, surrounded by books and papers. Head down, she was writing something in a red folder.

"I take everything back," said Rosa. "Jody is doing her book report after all."

When Jody saw her friends walking toward her she waved.

"Henry! Rosa! Darlings! Over here," she said, trying to sound like a movie star.

"I'm glad to see you're doing your book report," said Rosa.

Jody laughed. "Book report! That's not what I'm doing." She pushed a big green book across the table. "I'm just taking notes."

Rosa looked down at the book. It was called *Zombies on Parade*.

"What's this?" asked Rosa. She opened it up and saw a scary picture. It was from a movie called *Return of the Zombies*. In the picture, a man with a face like green jelly was holding a skull.

"Yuck!" said Rosa. "What are you reading this for?"

"I'm going to learn everything I can about zombies," said Jody. "That way I can have a super-real costume. When it comes to zombies I'm going to be super-smart."

"You're super-smart about a lot of things," said Henry. He pointed to Jody's folder. "Just look at your notes. You're making an outline. That's just what Ms. Hatfield told us to do."

"And you wrote the name of the book and the author at the top of the page. Ms. Hatfield told us to do that too," said Rosa. "You're real smart. I think you just don't realize it."

Jody's rubber four-leaf clover was out on the table. It was dark green and not much bigger than a quarter. She rubbed her finger along the clover and sighed. "I'm sorry. There's just no time to do that report."

"But you have to do it," said Rosa.

"It will have to wait," said Jody. "My costume is more important."

Rosa sighed. "But you don't want to stay back." She looked around the room then lowered her voice. "I have a friend who almost stayed back. It was terrible."

"What friend?" asked Jody.

24

Rosa looked around again. She bit at her lip. "I can't tell you," she said. "It's a secret."

"I wish I could stay in school," said Jody, "but I can't. Tommy Lee Turner needs me."

Jody looked down at the table. Suddenly her stomach began to hurt. Even thinking about school made her nervous. If only she were smart. If only school were easy, the way it was for Henry and Rosa.

"If you leave we'll miss you," said Henry. "You're our friend."

Jody forced a smile.

Henry reached into his pocket. "I've got something for you," he said. "It's a going-away present."

Jody looked up. She batted her eyelids and put a hand on her heart. "A present? For me?"

"Just for you," said Henry.

Jody looked at her clover. Maybe this was her lucky day after all. She smiled, shut her eyes, and held out her hand.

"I think you're going to like this," said Henry. He pulled a fat purple worm from his pocket and dropped it into Jody's hand. "Here, so that you'll always remember me."

Jody's eyes fluttered open. Then they nearly popped.

25

"Yikes! Yeow!" she screamed. "It's a . . . a creepy crawly thingy!"

The worm went flying. Jody leapt to her feet. Her papers tumbled to the floor like giant snowflakes.

"Wait a minute," cried Henry. He waved his arms at Jody, but she didn't see him. Her hands were over her eyes.

"Yi . . . Yi . . . Yiiikes!" she screamed.

"Jody, calm down. It's not real," said Henry.

"Shhhh!" said the librarian.

"Quiet!" said a girl at the next table.

Jody peeked out from between her fingers. She swallowed and stole a look at Henry's plastic worm lying on the floor.

"See," said Henry. "It's fake." He grinned and puffed out his chest. "Pretty neat, huh?"

Jody's face went red as a stoplight. She pointed a shaking finger at the door. "Out!" she screamed. "Leave!"

Henry looked confused.

"Does this mean you don't like my present?"

"Go!" screamed Jody.

Chapter 6

◆

Tommy Lee Turner

Tuesday night.

After dinner Jody read *Zombies on Parade* and took some more notes.

Then, at eight, she put away the book, got out her good-luck clover, and turned on the TV.

It was time for *My Zombie Boyfriend.*

Jody's little brother was already in bed. Her parents hated the show. So she got to watch it by herself. Just the way she liked it.

Tommy Lee Turner was soon on the screen. He had a red scar across his green cheek. His hair was purple. And he was dressed in rags, except for his white gloves.

"He's so cute," sighed Jody. She shut her

eyes and squeezed her rubber four-leaf clover. "I can hardly wait till we're good
friends."

Tommy Lee Turner was walking down a
street. He was holding a girl's hand.

"Soon that girl will be me," thought Jody.
"No more school. No more upset stom-
achs. No more dummy pants." She sighed
again. "Just me and Tommy Lee Turner."

Up on the TV Tommy Lee Turner was
saying good-bye to the girl. They were
standing outside an old tumbledown house.
The Zombie Boyfriend had to go home.

"I'm going to miss you," said the girl.
Her eyes were full of tears. Her long hair
was blowing in the breeze.

"I'll miss you too," said Tommy.

Jody thought about the things she would
miss if she went to Hollywood. She would
miss her parents. She would miss her friends
in the Creepy Creature Club. And she would
even miss Henry and his dumb jokes. But
most of all she would miss Rosa, her best
friend.

"I'll never have a friend like Rosa," she
thought. "Never again."

Tommy Lee Turner blew a kiss to his
girlfriend. Then he shivered. A cold wind

rattled the house's front door. He hated the old house, but it was his home.

"I wish I was smarter," said Jody to herself. "Then I could stay. I wouldn't have to run away." She squeezed her four-leaf clover. Hard.

Tommy Lee Turner went up the walk. "See you soon," he said. Then he just faded away.

Jody waved at the TV. "I'll see you soon too," she said. But she wasn't so excited about it. Not anymore. Not after she had thought about what she was going to have to give up.

She slammed her hand down on the arm of the chair. "I don't want to leave school," she cried. "I want to be smart." She sniffled. "If only I knew how."

Chapter 7

◆

Heading for Hollywood

Wednesday.

Jody brought her book, *Zombies on Parade,* to the cafeteria.

All during lunch she took notes. She read about zombies. And she read about other monsters too. For instance, she learned that Vlad was the real name of Count Dracula and he had once lived in Europe. His castle had been in Transylvania, which was part of the country of Romania. The book said Transylvania was near the Carpathian Mountains.

Reading about monsters was fun. Before long Jody had filled six pages in her red folder. All her facts were carefully outlined. She didn't realize it, but it was just the way

Ms. Hatfield had told the class to do their book reports.

Suddenly someone said, "What a surprise! I didn't know you could read."

Jody looked up. It was Angie Dobbs. She had a grin on her face and a plate in her hand. The plate was full of creamed corn.

"Are you really reading," said Angie, "or just looking at the pictures?"

Jody swallowed. She felt her stomach start to tighten. She reached into her pocket and squeezed her clover. "Angie, please. Leave me alone. I'm busy."

Angie put down her plate and leaned across the table.

"*Zombies on Parade!*" she said, looking at the book. "You must be trying for Ms. Hatfield's prize. I heard the winner gets to be on *My Zombie Boyfriend.*"

Jody closed the book. She eyed the creamed corn, wondering how it would look in Angie's hair.

"I'm going to make a great costume," said Angie. "You don't stand a chance. Anyway, you have to be smart to be on TV. They'll never pick a dummy pants. Not in a zillion years."

That did it. Jody reached for the creamed

corn. But before she could get to it a big ugly blob suddenly landed on the table.

Splat!

Jody glanced up. There were Henry and Rosa.

"What do you think?" said Henry. He pointed to the thing on the table. "Pretty neat, huh?"

Angie looked down, then gagged. "Oh, no, gross!"

"It almost looks real, doesn't it?" said Henry proudly.

"Yuck! It's throw-up!" yelled Angie. She scrunched up her face. She looked as if she had just eaten a sour lemon. Whole.

"Ooooo, get it away!" said Jody.

"Girls, it's only plastic," said Henry. "I bought it yesterday. At the joke shop."

"Some joke!" said Angie. She shivered. "Yuck! Barf-a-roo!"

Henry held out his hands. "What's wrong? Gee, I thought you'd like it."

Angie's face was the color of the creamed corn. "Henry, you're the sickest kid in this whole school!"

Henry smiled. He liked being the greatest, even if it was the greatest sicko.

Angie grabbed her stomach and wobbled away, muttering.

"Gee, I don't think she liked it," said Henry.

Rosa put her hands on Henry's shoulders. She looked into his face with her big brown eyes. "When people are eating they don't want to see your throw-up. Even if it is just plastic."

"Oh," said Henry, nodding. He picked up the glob of throw-up and turned it over in his hands. "I get it."

"You ruined Angie's meal," said Rosa.

"I'm glad you did," said Jody. "That girl is a creep."

"What did she say this time?" asked Rosa. She pulled up a chair and sat down next to her friend.

"She called me names," said Jody softly. "She said I was a dummy pants."

"She was just being mean," said Henry. He twirled the throw-up on his finger. "You're really very smart."

Jody tried not to look at the throw-up. "Thank you for saying that, but I know it's not true. I get the worst grades in class."

Rosa patted Jody on the shoulder. "That's

just because you're afraid to try. You don't do your work."

"I can't do my work," said Jody. "That's why I'm going to run away to Hollywood. Then I won't have to do that stupid book report."

"Jody, you have to do that report," said Rosa. "Do you want to stay back?"

Jody bit her lip. She looked like she was about to cry.

"I bet if you tried you'd do a great report," said Henry. He tossed the plastic yuck into the air and caught it on his forehead. "Be cool. Like me."

Jody stared at the table. "Reports are easy for you guys to do," she said. "You're smart."

Henry smiled. He couldn't argue with Jody. He thought he was the smartest kid in school. Maybe in the whole world.

But Rosa said, "We're not any smarter than you. We just do our work. You could get good grades too. You just have to try."

"That's easy for you to say," said Jody.

Rosa looked around. Then she put her hand on top of Jody's. "Last year I got bad grades too. Mr. Hayes told my parents I might have to stay back."

37

"Really?" said Jody. She looked up. "You never told me this before."

"I never told anyone," said Rosa.

"So, what happened?" asked Henry. He let the throw-up slide off his forehead into his hand.

"I started to do my work," said Rosa. "Just like Jody, I was afraid to try." She patted Jody's hand. "It turned out it wasn't that hard. It was even fun."

Jody sat quietly for a while. At last she sighed and shook her head. "But I don't know how to do a book report."

"Of course you do," said Rosa. She pointed to Jody's red folder. "You're doing one right there. You've outlined *Zombies on Parade* and everything."

"But *Zombies on Parade* isn't a real book," she said. "It's too weird for Ms. Hatfield."

"So, then do something else," said Henry.

"There's not enough time," said Jody. She gathered up her stuff and got to her feet. "Face it. I'm just not smart enough."

"Nonsense. You're as smart as anyone," said Rosa.

"That isn't what Angie says," said Jody.

"Angie isn't your friend," said Rosa.

Jody started to leave. "Angie isn't my

38

friend," she said, over her shoulder, "but she is honest. When she says I'm a dummy pants she's right. Everyone knows it."

Henry watched Jody walk away. When she turned around he waved to her with his plastic goo.

"Poor girl," he said, shaking his head. "I think she's already made up her mind. She's heading for Hollywood."

"That girl isn't heading for Hollywood," said Rosa. "She's heading for trouble."

Chapter 8

◆

Transylvania

Thursday.

Jody spent the afternoon in class thinking about Hollywood. It wasn't really a daydream. It was more like a "daymare," a bad dream. In the dream she was trapped far from friends and family. People were laughing. They were calling her dummy pants because she had quit school.

In front Ms. Hatfield was talking about geography. "Yesterday we studied maps," she said. "I want to find out what you learned."

Everyone looked up. Everyone but Jody. She took out her red folder. It was stuffed with papers. She looked at a drawing she had made of a zombie. Then she looked at what she had written about some famous monsters.

She was reading about Dracula when she heard someone call her name.

"Jody! I'm asking you a question." Jody looked up. It was Ms. Hatfield. Quickly she closed the folder.

"Yes," she said.

"You weren't paying attention, were you?" Ms. Hatfield looked over the top of her glasses. "Shall I repeat the question?"

Jody gulped. "Yes, please."

Ms. Hatfield sighed. "Did you study your maps last night?"

"Yes," lied Jody.

"Well," said Ms. Hatfield, "then tell me something about the country of Romania."

"Um, Romania?" asked Jody. The name seemed familiar. But she couldn't remember where she'd heard of it before.

From somewhere behind her Jody heard Angie Dobbs whisper, "Jody Grimes doesn't know where Romania is. She's so dumb she doesn't even know where her nose is."

"Shut up, Angie!" said Rosa.

Ms. Hatfield cleared her throat. She stared over the top of her glasses. "Romania. Where is it?"

41

Suddenly, Jody remembered where she'd learned about Romania. In her zombie book!

"Romania," she said. "It's in Europe. Count Dracula came from there. He lived in Transylvania. That's near the Car- ... Car- ..." She clapped her hands together. "The Carpathian Mountains!"

"Wow," said Henry. "Even I didn't know all that."

Ms. Hatfield grinned. "Ms. Grimes, I think you've been studying."

Jody felt wonderful. She reached into her pocket and squeezed her four-leaf clover. Everyone in the class was talking about her answer. She felt smart!

"Cheater," said Angie Dobbs.

"I'm not a cheater," said Jody, glaring. "Or a dummy pants either."

Angie grumbled and turned away.

Suddenly, school felt like fun to Jody. She was sorry it was her last week. Too bad, she thought. Too bad I'll be a big movie star soon and have to leave.

Chapter 9

◆

White Gloves

After school Jody hurried to the Creepy Creature clubhouse. She needed to pick up some things there. Things for her zombie costume.

She gave the secret password and went inside.

Most of the club members were busy working on their Halloween costumes. After all, tomorrow was the big day. As Jody crossed the room she passed by Rosa the witch, Melvin the ghost, and Darlene, made up like a green-faced zombie.

"Good costume. But not good enough," said Jody. She patted Darlene on the shoulder with her red folder. "My zombie costume is going to be ten times better."

The only one who wasn't wearing a costume was Henry. He was sitting at the table counting out his money.

"Hello," said Henry. "I thought you would be working on your report. I'm surprised to see you."

"I just came by to get some white gloves," said Jody. "I think there are some in the clothes box."

On the floor at the end of the table was a big cardboard box. It was full of dress-up clothes. All kinds of things were in there. Funny hats, scarfs, shoes, even jewelry.

Henry fiddled with the coins in his hand. "What do you need gloves for?" he asked. "I thought zombies only wore dirty, ripped-up shirts and pants."

"Most zombies do. But not Tommy Lee Turner," said Jody. She put her red folder on the table. Then she stuck her head in the clothes box and dug in. "On *My Zombie Boyfriend* Tommy always wears white gloves. So I want some too. What's wrong, don't you ever watch that show?"

"I've got better things to do," said Henry.

Jody looked up from the box. "Like what? Buy stupid stuff at the joke shop?"

"In fact that's just where I'm going," said

45

Henry. He shoved the coins in his pocket. "I'm going to get something really great."

Jody didn't look up. "Like what?"

"A surprise," said Henry. "I'll show you tomorrow."

At last Jody fished out a pair of white gloves.

"I knew they were in here," she said. She held them up proudly. "Look. Aren't they just perfect?"

Rosa put on a witch's hat and walked over to the table. "Jody," she said, lowering her voice. "Did you do your report for Ms. Hatfield?"

Jody bit her lip. Then she sighed and patted her red folder. "This is the only report I need," she said. "It has made me a zombie expert. And tomorrow it's going to make me a star."

"Tomorrow Ms. Hatfield is going to make you a stay-back," said Rosa. She tapped her forehead. "In fact, I predict it if you don't do your report."

Jody looked down. She twisted the gloves in her hand. "I can't do that report."

"Sure you can," said Rosa. "You're smart. You knew all about Romania, didn't you?"

"That was different," said Jody.

"Please. Just try," said Rosa.

Jody smiled. It was a sad little smile. "Sorry. Even if I wanted to do a report I couldn't. There's not enough time." She pulled on her gloves. "I have no choice. I have to go to Hollywood."

"But that's not true," said Rosa.

"Please don't worry about me," said Jody. She started for the door. "I know exactly what I'm doing."

"Jody.... You're making a mistake!" cried Rosa.

"Bye-bye, friends," said Jody. She stopped at the door and blew everyone a kiss. "Wish me luck."

"She's going to need it," said Rosa to Henry, "because only luck will save her now."

Chapter *10*

◆

A Class of Monsters

Friday.

Everyone came to school in costume. The room was full of monsters. Rosa the witch was there. So was Henry the ghost, with a sheet over his head. In the front row sat a giant ape, a vampire, and a warty-faced creature from Mars.

Four zombies had shown up too. The only one that looked as scary as Jody was Angie. She had a drippy green face and a big red eyeball hanging off her cheek. Like Jody, she was wearing a pair of snow-white gloves.

"Where did you get that lousy costume?" asked Angie. "Did you buy it at Zombies R Us?"

"You can laugh now," said Jody. "But you won't be laughing later." She patted her red folder. "I might not be good at book reports, but when it comes to zombies I'm an expert."

Jody did have on a great costume. She had spent all week working on it. It showed. Her face was streaked with green and purple. Her clothes were torn and looked to be covered with blood. Her hair was caked with dirt. She was a mess. Except, of course, for her Tommy Lee Turner gloves. Her white, white gloves.

She held up her gloves and blew on them. "I'm the best zombie in the world," she said. "Admit it, Angie. I am."

"Don't make me laugh," said Angie. She started to walk away, then stopped and pointed. "Face it, Jody. You're a loser. You're a loser in school. And you're going to be a loser today."

Even Ms. Hatfield was dressed up. She was wearing her monster cape and a pointed black witch's hat.

"Happy Halloween," said Ms. Hatfield as soon as the bell had rung. As soon as everyone was seated.

"Happy Halloween!" said the class.

"Today someone will win a special prize," said Ms. Hatfield. She was leaning against her desk. "Someone with a very special costume."

"That's me," thought Jody. She put her rubber four-leaf clover on her desk. Then she patted it for luck.

"The winner is going to be on television," said Ms. Hatfield. "That's the special prize I told you about."

"Big surprise," whispered Jody. "We already knew that."

Melvin Purdy raised his hand. "When will the television show be here?"

"Right after lunch," said Ms. Hatfield. "They'll be here when you come back. They'll take pictures of all of you. Then they'll pick the one they want on their show."

"What show is it?" asked Jody.

"You'll see," said Ms. Hatfield. "After lunch."

Jody looked around the room at all the monsters. "This is my last day in class," she thought. "I'll never see Rosa or Henry or Melvin again." Jody felt bad about leaving her friends. "I'm going to miss them. Especially Rosa." She sighed and ran her finger along her red folder. "If only I were smarter. If only I had done a book report."

The morning dragged by. Ms. Hatfield let people talk quietly or read. Ten o'clock came. Then eleven.

At last it was noon.

The bell rang. Everyone ran out the door. Everyone but Jody.

She was still in her seat. She wanted to read one last thing in her folder. It was something she had copied out of *Zombies on Parade*. It told how a zombie walks.

"They often drag one leg," it said, "and walk slowly, keeping their eyes straight ahead."

"Jody?" said Ms. Hatfield.

Jody looked up. Ms. Hatfield was standing in the aisle.

"It's lunchtime," said Ms. Hatfield. She reached down and tapped the red folder. "You know your book report is due today. Is this it?"

Jody looked at the folder, then up at Ms. Hatfield.

"Huh?" she said.

"This red folder. Is it your book report?" asked Ms. Hatfield again.

Jody ran her finger down the folder and

thought. Yes. Maybe she had written a book report. She had outlined. She had put the author's name and the title at the top. She had done all the things Ms. Hatfield had told the class to do.

She thought some more. Yes. Yes! It was a book report. And a pretty good one too. A dummy pants couldn't have found out so much about zombies. Or written it down so well. Only a smarty pants could have. Someone who would know where Romania was. Someone like her.

Ms. Hatfield picked up the folder. "May I look at it?"

Jody swallowed. For a moment she thought about taking it back. "It's kind of a weird report," she said.

"It looks like a long report," said Ms. Hatfield. "You must have worked very hard on it."

"It took me all week," said Jody. "But you know what? It wasn't hard at all. It was fun."

"Schoolwork is supposed to be fun," said Ms. Hatfield.

"That's what Rosa said too," said Jody. "It's taken me a long time to learn that." She looked at the folder and thought again about taking it back. "I hope it's good enough," she added.

Ms. Hatfield held onto the folder. "I'm looking forward to reading it." She smiled. "Now you'd better get to lunch. The cook told me that she's made a special Halloween meal."

Jody got to her feet. She glanced back at Ms. Hatfield. She hoped she didn't laugh at her report.

Ms. Hatfield smiled. "I like your costume," she said.

Jody returned Ms. Hatfield's smile. Then she headed for the door, slowly. Eyes straight ahead, one leg dragging behind. Off to lunch she went. Like a zombie.

Chapter *11*

◆

Pumpkin Pie

Ms. Hatfield was right. Lunch was special. Hamburgers, with the buns decorated like jack-o'-lanterns. French fries, dyed orange. And pumpkin pie. Two whole pumpkin pies in the middle of each table.

Mrs. Ames, the cook, had painted blue freckles on her cheeks. "The pies are for dessert," she said. "Make sure you share."

Jody took a hamburger and french fries. Then she found a seat and sat down across from a ghost. When the ghost took off its sheet she saw that it was Henry.

He picked up a hamburger with one hand and a fistful of french fries with the other. "Ummm," he said. "I wish every day was Halloween."

"What a pig," thought Jody.

"Good food, huh?" said Henry, between bites.

"I wouldn't know," said Jody. "I'm not eating."

Henry's mouth was stuffed with food. But that didn't stop him from speaking. "Not eating? Aren't you hungry?"

"Too nervous," said Jody. She held up her hands. "Besides, I can't afford to get my gloves dirty."

"It's unhealthy to skip lunch," mumbled Henry. His cheeks were puffed out like a chipmunk's. "Why not take off the gloves?"

Jody smiled through purple lips. "I can't take them off. I might get makeup on them. They have to be spotless. They have to look just like Tommy Lee Turner's."

Henry licked his lips. "Does that mean I can have your hamburger?"

Henry had a piece of french fry stuck on his chin. "Aren't you full?" said Jody. "Don't you want to save room for the pie?"

Henry turned his attention to the two fat pies sitting between Jody and him. He chewed on his food for a while and thought.

"I'll have room," he finally said. "Let me have your food."

Jody turned up her nose. "No," she said. "You've already had enough."

Henry pulled back his head. The piece of french fry dropped off his chin. "What?"

Jody tugged at her gloves. "I said no. I don't want you to get sick."

Henry ran his tongue around the inside of his mouth.

He stared at Jody but didn't speak. All the while he was thinking.

Finally he reached into his pocket and pulled out a little plastic bottle.

"Guess what I bought yesterday?" he said.

Jody narrowed her eyes. "Not some stupid trick, I hope."

Henry held up the bottle. "A trick? Does this look like a trick? This happens to be a bottle of the world's most expensive perfume."

Jody raised an eyebrow. "Perfume?"

Just then Henry saw Angie Dobbs. "Hey, Angie!" he called. "Want some perfume? Jody doesn't want it."

Angie came walking over. "What kind of perfume?" she asked.

"French perfume," said Henry. "It cost me a lot."

"French perfume?" said Jody. Suddenly

58

she was interested again. "You know, movie stars wear French perfume."

"Do you want to try some?" said Henry.

"I thought you said I could have it," said Angie. She put her white gloves on her hips. "You asked me first."

Henry raised a hand. "Please. There's enough for both of you. Jody, do you want some too?"

Jody batted her eyelashes. "Well, I guess a little wouldn't hurt."

"Yes, just a little," said Angie. She held out her hands. "Not too much. On my wrists."

Jody held out her hands too. "Go ahead. Give me some of that expensive perfume." She giggled. "There's no reason a zombie has to smell bad."

Jody shut her eyes. So did Angie. Then Henry squirted the bottle onto their gloves. Instead of perfume, out came a stream of black ink. In a second the girls' gloves were covered with black spots.

"Surprise!" said Henry.

Jody's eyes popped open. When she saw her gloves she almost fainted. Angie too. Her mouth was open. She tried to scream but nothing came out.

59

Henry laughed. "It's only a joke," he said. "I got it yesterday at the joke shop."

"How ... how could you!" screamed Jody. "My gloves. They're filthy!"

Everyone in the cafeteria turned to see what was going on.

Henry held up his hands. "Jody, Angie, wait. It's just a trick...."

Without thinking Jody grabbed a pumpkin pie. She drew back her hand and aimed for Henry's face.

"Whoa!" shouted Henry. "The ink isn't real. It's disappearing ..."

Splat! Before Henry could explain that the ink wasn't real. That it would fade away in thirty seconds. That her gloves would be white again. Before he could say any of that, the pie hit him smack in the face.

"That's what you get!" screamed Jody. Already the ink was fading on her gloves. But she didn't notice. She was mad. Real mad. Mad enough to throw another pie. If she'd had one.

But she didn't have another pie. That's because Angie had it.

Splat! It smashed right into Henry's face.

"Henry Potter!" screamed Angie. "You ruined my costume!"

Henry was stunned. Gobs of pumpkin pie, like leaky orange warts, covered his face. He got to his feet and licked some pie off his lips.

Everyone in the cafeteria was laughing. Everyone but Mrs. Ames. She came charging out from behind the counter.

"What's going on!" she roared.

Henry didn't wait to see what she was going to do. He took off. Though one eye was covered with pie he saw his way out the cafeteria door. Then across the playground he ran.

"There are some paper towels in the classroom," he said to himself. "Maybe I can clean up before everyone gets back."

The classroom door was wide open. He charged through.

"Eyyyahhhh!" he screamed. "Out of my way!"

Halfway to the paper towels he realized he wasn't alone. In fact, the room was full. Besides Ms. Hatfield, there were about ten other men and women standing around. Big bright lights were shining down from tall stands. TV cameras were everywhere.

"Oh-oh," thought Henry.

"Great!" shouted a woman in a dark dress. She was holding a pad of paper in one hand. "Did we get that on tape?"

"We got it, Ms. Oliver," said a tall man behind one of the cameras. "I've never seen such a real-looking zombie."

Henry rubbed some of the pie off his cheek. "Zombie?" he said.

"Isn't that what you are?" asked the woman, Ms. Oliver. "That's great makeup you're wearing."

"Actually, it's—" began Henry.

"Now, what's your name?" interrupted Ms. Oliver. "I think you may be the one we want for our show."

Henry gulped. "Me? Really?"

"Of course, we'll have to look at the other kids too," she said. She shook her head. "Yuck! What is that stuff on your face?"

Henry smiled. "It's a secret," he said.

Lunch had just ended. All the kids were beginning to head back to class. In the distance came Angie and Jody. Their gloves were white. Perfectly white. Once again.

"A secret?" said Ms. Oliver. "You won't tell?"

Henry shook his head. "A zombie never tells," he said. "Maybe my makeup girl will tell you though."

Jody suddenly appeared in the doorway.

"Ah," said Henry, "there she is now."

63

Chapter 12

♦

A Class Star

Jody had been running, but the second she saw the lights and the cameras and all the people, she slowed down.

She let her leg drag behind her. Moaning, she entered the room.

"Beware," she called. "The zombie walks tonight."

"Come, come on in," said Ms. Oliver. "You look great."

Jody dragged herself through the door. All the while her eyes were searching the room. She was looking for Tommy Lee Turner.

"He must be hiding somewhere," she thought.

She touched a finger to her forehead and

pulled herself up to Ms. Hatfield's desk. "I have risen from the grave!" she said. "Now I must search for my Zombie Boyfriend."

"Jody!" said Ms. Hatfield. "What are you talking about?"

"My Zombie Boyfriend," said Jody. Now she looked about the room desperately. "Where are you? Appear!"

When no one appeared Jody looked around, confused.

"Where's Tommy Lee Turner?" she asked.

"Tommy Lee Turner? The actor?" said Ms. Oliver.

"Yes," said Jody. "Couldn't he make it?"

Ms. Oliver wrinkled her brow. "What?"

Everyone was staring at Jody. "But ... aren't you all from the TV show *My Zombie Boyfriend*?"

The woman laughed. "Do we look that strange? No, sweetheart," she said, "we're from the six o'clock news."

Ms. Hatfield stepped forward. "Since it's Halloween, the news tonight will begin with a picture of a scary monster." Ms. Hatfield waved her hand around the room. "One of you."

Jody was upset. But only for a moment. After all, she still had a chance to be on

65

TV. Even if it was just for a moment. Even if it was just the news.

All the people from the TV show held a meeting. At last they said, "We've decided to use the screaming zombie," said a man in a bright-green suit.

Jody wiggled her head. She acted embarrassed. "You mean me?"

"Of course not," said Angie. She was standing by the door. "He means me."

"No, I'm sorry," said the man. "We're talking about that zombie over there." He pointed at Henry. "The one with the warty orange face."

"Henry!" said Angie. "That's not fair."

"That's not makeup on his face," said Jody. "It's only pumpkin pie."

Henry held out his hands. "Well, there goes the secret. My makeup artist has spilled the beans."

Jody tore off her white, white gloves. She threw them on the floor. Then she ran to her seat. And put her head down on her desk.

"Did we do something wrong?" asked Ms. Oliver.

Ms. Hatfield smiled. "Not at all," she said. She followed Jody to her desk. She patted her on the back.

"Jody, I want to tell you that you've made me very proud today," said Ms. Hatfield.

Jody sniffled.

"I'm serious," said Ms. Hatfield. "Today you're my best student."

That got Jody's attention. She lifted up her head. "Best student? Me?"

Ms. Hatfield smiled. "Your book report was excellent. Filled with so many facts. And drawings. It was the best in the class."

"Book report?" said Jody. In all the excitement she had forgotten about the report.

"Yes, your book report. *Zombies on Parade.*" Ms. Hatfield set the red folder on Jody's desk. "I read it while you were at lunch."

Jody looked down at the folder. "It wasn't too weird?"

"Not at all," said Ms. Hatfield. "In fact, it was the most complete report I've ever seen." She put her hand on Jody's shoulder. "You're a very smart girl. But I think it took you a long time to realize it."

Jody grinned. "So you really liked my report?"

"You're a star," said Ms. Hatfield. "I'm very proud of you."

Just then Rosa and Henry walked up to Jody's desk.

"Are you feeling better?" asked Rosa.

"Much better," said Jody. "Ms. Hatfield likes my book report."

"Book report?" said Rosa.

"Yes. My report on *Zombies on Parade,*" said Jody. "The one I worked on all week."

"I told you so," said Rosa. "All this time you weren't just learning about zombies, you were doing a report. You just didn't believe in yourself. You didn't believe you could do it."

Jody picked up her four-leaf clover. She turned it over in her hands. "I guess this brought me luck after all."

"It wasn't luck that wrote that report. It was hard work. Your hard work," said Rosa. "You did it, not your clover."

Jody smiled up at Rosa. "Thanks for showing me that schoolwork could be fun."

"You taught yourself a lesson too," said Rosa. "You taught yourself that you were smart."

"Sounds like Jody has learned a lot," said Henry. "I think we'll have to start calling her smarty pants."

"I won't mind a bit," said Jody. She smiled.

"You know what? My stomach doesn't hurt anymore. I think that means I like school."

"Next year we'll all be together," said Rosa. She shut her eyes and raised a finger. "In fact, I predict it!"

Jody laughed. Then she put a finger on her forehead. "Now let me predict something," she said. "I see a girl and a boy, Rosa and Henry. They're going to be my best friends. Now and forever."

"That's a great prediction," said Henry. "I really mean it."

"I believe you," said Rosa. "And I know you're not joking either."

"Of course I'm not joking. I'm Henry," said Henry.

Rosa rolled her eyes at Henry's dumb joke. "Some people never change," she said.

Monster Jokes

Hi! It's Henry Potter. Everyone knows how brave, smart, and cute I am. But did you know I'm also very, very funny? I don't like to brag, but I know some of the best monster jokes anywhere. See for yourself. Here are just a few of my better ones:

What does a ghost wear around his neck?
A Boo Tie.

What did the monster have for breakfast?
Scream of wheat.

What is it called when a ghost makes a mistake?
A boo-boo.

What is Dracula's favorite kind of dog?
A bloodhound.

Why did the teacher kick Dracula out of her class?
Because he was a pain in the neck.

Nutty Ned: Doctor, I'm worried. I keep thinking I'm a pair of curtains.
Doctor: Stop worrying and pull yourself together.

How many dead people are in a cemetery?
All of them.

Little Monster: Dad, would you do my math for me?
Dad: No, my son, it wouldn't be right.
Little Monster: Come on, Dad, at least you could try.

Little Monster: Mommy, why do you have so many gray hairs?
Mommy: Probably because you're so bad and always cause me to worry.
Little Monster: I guess you must have been terrible to Grandma.

What did the mother ghost say to her daughter?
Stop goblin your food.